Weekly Reader Books presents

Mishmash

and the Big Fat Problem

MOLLY CONE

Illustrated by Leonard Shortall

HOUGHTON MIFFLIN COMPANY BOSTON 1982

My thanks to Jeannie Wright and
her Healthy Heart Club of
Suquamish Elementary School for
sharing their workouts with me.
And my thanks also to Weight
Watchers International for the use
of their name in this book.

This book a presentation of
Weekly Reader Books.

Weekly Reader Books offers book clubs for children
from preschool through junior high school.
All quality hardcover books are selected by
a distinguished Weekly Reader Selection Board.

For further information write to:
Weekly Reader Books
1250 Fairwood Ave.
Columbus, Ohio 43216

Printed in the United States of America
Library of Congress Cataloging in Publication Data
Cone, Molly.
Mishmash and the big fat problem.
Summary: When Mishmash the dog becomes overweight,
Pete and Wanda try hypnosis and an exercise routine to
get him slim again.
[1. Dogs – Fiction.   2. Weight control – Fiction]
I. Shortall, Leonard W., ill.   II. Title.
PZ7.C7592Mim   [Fic]   81-20216
ISBN 0-395-32078-X   AACR2

1

"What's all that thumping and jumping I heard coming from your room this morning?" Pete's father called from his radish patch. "You're not keeping some animal up there, are you?"

"Animal? What animal?" said Pete, coming out of the house. He sat on the back porch step to tighten the laces of his running shoes.

His father meant Mishmash, of course. The teacher's dog. But Pete hadn't seen much of Mishmash lately. He hadn't had any time to play with Mishmash. He was too busy doing push ups and stomach curls and straddle stretches, and running around the field at school.

Mr. Peters set the nozzle of the hose at a fine spray and turned his glance toward Pete.

"It was only me," Pete said quickly. "I was doing my loosener-uppers."

Mr. Peters went back to watering his garden. "Some new game you're playing?"

"It's not a game," said Pete.

"It's his homework," said Mrs. Peters, who had just come around the corner of the house with a potted rosebush. She set it down on the porch steps and regarded it lovingly. "First Lady," she said. "It's yellow and pink."

"Homework?" Pete's father squinted over his shoulder at the two of them. "What happened to arithmetic? And history? Doesn't anyone do homework on arithmetic and spelling and history anymore? It seems to me that schools used to teach things out of books."

Mrs. Peters picked up a trowel and began digging a hole by the side of the steps.

"It's for our health class," said Pete. "We're having a six-day runathon during spring vacation.

The whole school is doing it. The team in each room that does the most miles gets an award."

"Is that so?" said Mr. Peters. He bent to secure the empty seed envelope that was stuck onto a stick. On it was a picture of a large round radish. The label read *Giant Scarlet Globe*.

"Wanda is captain of her Healthy Heart team, and I'm captain of mine," Pete told his father. He couldn't help frowning.

Mr. Peters turned the nozzle to shut off the water entirely. "Well, that explains it," he said, and started toward the garden faucet.

"It doesn't explain anything!" Pete shouted after him.

His mother stopped digging. "It wouldn't hurt you to be a little nicer to Wanda," she said just as the slam of a door echoed across the yard.

Pete turned around. Wanda was coming down her back steps with a clipboard in her hands.

Wanda Sparling lived in the house next door. At school Wanda sat in the seat next to Pete. In the lunchroom she always elbowed into line in front of him. On the playground she often grabbed the ball he was getting ready to catch. The only thing she had never beaten him at was arithmetic. Pete was better than Wanda at anything having to do with arithmetic.

"Hi, Wanda," Pete said loudly, just to show how nice he could be.

Wanda tapped her pencil importantly on the clipboard. "I came over to speak to your mother," she said in the voice she used for selling Girl Scout cookies.

Mrs. Peters straightened up. "Hello, Wanda."

Her smile was far too kind, Pete thought. But he smiled at Wanda too, just to show his mother that he could.

Wanda smiled back. It was the kind of smile TV announcers make when telling you to get ready for a commercial.

"Mrs. Peters, I'm giving you the opportunity to sponsor my team in our Healthy Heart Runathon."

Pete smothered a laugh.

Wanda went right on talking to his mother. "All you have to do is pledge five cents a mile for every mile my team runs when we win."

"*When* you win?" said Pete, forgetting all about being nice. "Did you say *when* you win?"

Wanda only smiled more brightly at Mrs. Peters. "We already have five sponsors —"

Pete hooted. Five sponsors meant five parents of the five team members.

"And you may rest assured that your money will go to a good cause."

"What cause?" Pete demanded.

"Jogging shoes," Wanda said promptly. "For Miss Patch. It's going to be a present from my team. But it was my idea," she quickly added.

"It sounds like a very nice idea, Wanda," said Mrs. Peters. "And certainly — unusual."

Pete paid no attention to Wanda's triumphant smirk. He was beginning to wonder why Wanda was suddenly so interested in giving a present to their teacher. He gazed at her suspiciously.

"May I put you on my sponsor list?" Wanda's pencil poised over the paper attached to her clipboard.

"Well . . ." Mrs. Peters looked a little uncertainly from Wanda to Pete. "How many miles do you think that might be?"

"We'll probably go at least sixty," Wanda said rather loudly.

Sixty. Pete calculated swiftly. That meant two miles a day for every one of the five members of Wanda's team. Ten miles altogether, every day of the six days of the marathon.

He thought of the classmates on his team. Harry Hamilton, who was too fat to do more than a couple of times around the half-mile course. Sara Mayer, who would do all her running with a book stuck in front of her face if he didn't watch her. Adele Bittford, who stopped running as soon as she started to sweat. And Jules Ivar.

Pete stopped worrying when he thought of Jules. Jules was small and fast. He could pitch a ball farther, jump higher, and run faster than any kid in Pete's class. He was as good as a whole team all by himself. Sixty miles? Pete smiled.

"We don't believe we have any *real* competition," Wanda was saying to his mother. "That is, none to speak of."

"Hah!" said Pete.

Mrs. Peters picked up her trowel. "Well, I'll think about it, Wanda." She started toward the front of the house.

"I'll come back later," Wanda called after her. "I have to go over to Miss Patch's house to check on her shoe size."

Pete watched Wanda walk down the street with her clipboard stuck under her arm.

"Pete?" His father was down on his hands and knees, peering at his radish patch. "Come here a minute. I want to show you something."

Pete went over and stood beside him.

"Look." Mr. Peters waved his hand over the garden plot.

Pete looked. "I don't see anything."

"Look carefully," said his father patiently. "If you look extra sharp you can see two tiny leaves poking up."

"Two tiny leaves?" Pete squinted across the top of the soil. He didn't see any leaves.

"Pinhead size," said his father eagerly. "See them?"

Pete gazed at the ground, but in his mind he was picturing Wanda walking down the street toward the teacher's house. He saw her reach the teacher's gate. He saw her stepping up to the front door.

Suddenly he remembered that every time Wanda talked about giving anyone a present she had something else on her mind.

With a yell, Pete whirled and ran down the street after her.

2
————

Miss Patch opened the door. She was wearing her wrinkled jeans and old tennis shoes. Pete was pleased to see the sour look on Wanda's face when he arrived.

Suddenly he heard a roaring in his ears as a big black shape hurtled out to greet him. It was Mishmash, barking like crazy.

"Quiet!" said Miss Patch.

Mishmash snapped his mouth closed, but he kept on yipping and whining. He stood up on his hind legs, put his paws on Pete's shoulders, and slapped his tongue all over Pete's face.

"Yaccchh!" said Wanda.

"Hi, Mishmash." Pete patted and thumped him. "Hi, boy. How are you today? I haven't seen you for a long time."

"I'll tell you how he is today," Miss Patch said, her teeth sticking out. But she wasn't smiling her usual smile. "He's fatter than he was yesterday. That's how he is today."

Pete pushed the dog down and looked at him.

"He weighs ten pounds more than he did exactly one month ago!" said Miss Patch.

One month ago was when Pete had gotten interested in running. One month ago, Pete had started spending all his after-school time training. Pete frowned at the dog's bulging belly.

The grin slipped off Mishmash's face. His jowls bobbled. The big black head ducked, and the big feet took two clumsy steps backward.

"Owww!" said Wanda. "Get off my feet, you big lummox!"

Mishmash moved one of his hind legs and sat down heavily on the floor. His large head rested on his forepaws.

11

"He can't help it if he's got big feet," said Pete. "He's a big dog."

Wanda eyed the dog critically. "He's not big — he's just plain fat. He's even fatter than Harry Hamilton."

Pete glared at her. Pete hadn't chosen Harry Hamilton to be on his team. It just happened that way. No one got to choose teams. They had to draw colored slips of paper out of a bag. His team was green. Wanda's was yellow.

Mishmash got up and walked away. He went to the television set, batted it on with a swipe of his paw, and settled down before it.

"All he does is eat and watch television," said Miss Patch in a worried voice.

"My mother says that eating too much can become a habit," said Wanda. "She says that people who eat too much hardly even know they have a problem. She says that every time she wakes up and finds herself down in front of the refrigerator she knows it's a sign that something is wrong."

12

Miss Patch gave her head a little shake. "The vet says there is nothing wrong with Mishmash — except maybe boredom."

"You mean a dog can get bored?" said Wanda.

"Sure, a dog can get bored," Pete said quickly. "If he's smart." Pete couldn't help feeling a little proud. There was no denying that Mishmash was smart.

Wanda snorted. "Oh he's *smart* all right. He's *so* smart he stands up and drools every time he sees a food commercial on television."

Miss Patch began to look even more worried. "Do you think maybe he's watching too much television? Dogs are very impressionable, you know. Just as impressionable as kids."

Mishmash turned his head. He stared at Miss Patch for a moment, his eyes unblinking. Then he batted at the volume button. The sound blared, and the dog settled down again.

Wanda giggled. "You've insulted him," she said. "He probably thinks he's a lot smarter than any kid."

"Well, he is smarter," Pete said loyally. "He's smarter than most kids, anyway."

"Well, he's not smarter than *I* am," said Miss Patch. She clapped her hands together.

Mishmash looked up.

"Out!" She pointed to the door. "It's time you took a little exercise."

The dog didn't move.

"Come on, Mishmash." Pete took a step or two. "Let's go for a walk. We haven't taken a walk for a long time."

Miss Patch sniffed. "The only walk he thinks he needs is from the TV set to the refrigerator."

Mishmash pushed himself up. He gave the teacher a mournful look. Then he lumbered out the back door after Pete.

"Don't feed him anything!" Miss Patch shouted after them. "He's on a strict diet. He's not supposed to eat anything between meals."

Pete led the dog up the street. "You've got to stop making a pig of yourself. No more milk shakes." He scowled. "You understand?"

Mishmash dragged along beside Pete. He didn't even turn his head to listen.

"No more hamburgers, or French fries, or ice cream, or chocolate-chip cookies."

"No Slurpees," said Wanda breathlessly as she caught up with them. "And he can't have any pizza either. My mother goes to Weight Watchers, and she won't eat potato chips or pretzels or pancakes or waffles." Wanda sighed. "We've been eating fish almost every day, it seems."

Mishmash turned his head. His lip curled back. A low growl slipped out of his throat.

"Mishmash doesn't like fish," Pete said.

"Neither does my mother," said Wanda. "She says she's eaten so much fish already that she's sure she's growing fins and scales. She says if you could put all the fish she's eaten end to end, it would make her throw up." A snort came out of Mishmash's mouth. Or something that sounded like a snort.

Wanda kept right on talking. "She's lost ten

pounds. When she loses ten more she'll get a medal."

Pete looked doubtfully at Mishmash. "I don't think Mishmash cares much about medals," he said.

Wanda came to a stop. She gave a good imitation of a snort herself. "Nobody's going to give Mishmash any medals, I'll tell you that. Nobody in his right mind would even give Mishmash the time of day. My mother says that if he comes around sticking his head into our garbage can one more time, she's going to booby-trap it."

Pete stopped too. "How do you know it was Mishmash who got into your garbage can?"

Wanda snorted again — a real one this time, not an imitation. "Just look at him," she said.

Pete looked. Fat face, fat chin, buttery eyes. Pete was uncomfortably reminded of Harry Hamilton.

Mishmash's mouth stretched into a grin, and Pete frowned.

Wanda gave an elaborate shrug. "Well, I'm

glad it's not my problem." She gave him a pitying look. "I'm glad I'm not the one who is responsible for a dog like Mishmash. Lucky for me it wasn't my idea to foist a dog like that off on a teacher like Miss Patch."

"I didn't foist anything off on anyone!" Pete shouted. "He was a present. He was the best present she ever got!"

"I wouldn't count on that," Wanda said with a knowing look.

Pete followed her gaze. Mishmash was sitting on the curb licking a lollipop some kid had thrown into the gutter.

"MISHMASH!" yelled Pete.

Mishmash gulped. The lollipop disappeared. It went down his throat, stick and all.

3

Pete waited until he was sure Wanda had gone off to school before he started off. Then he hurried out the back door.

Mishmash was standing before the overturned garbage can. Empty cans and papers and apple peelings surrounded him.

"Mishmash!" Pete whispered hoarsely as he looked around quickly. "You're not supposed to be here."

The dog raised his head, blinked at Pete, and went back to licking at a discarded margarine wrapper.

Pete pulled it away from him. He uprighted the

garbage can, scooped the stuff back in, and hurriedly led Mishmash out of the yard.

"You're eating too much. D'you hear me? You're getting too fat."

The big black dog suddenly stopped trotting along beside Pete. He put his nose up in the air and sniffed.

"Mishmash!" called Pete.

Mishmash moved. But not in the direction Pete was headed. He raced back through the Sparlings' yard and disappeared around the corner of the house.

"Here, Mishmash. Here, Mishmash," Pete called.

The door of the house opened. Mrs. Sparling came out and shook out a dish towel. The smell of burnt toast came out with her.

"Hello, Pete," she said, and looked at him suspiciously. "What are you doing around here? Aren't you supposed to be on your way to school?"

Pete smiled politely. "I *am* on my way to

school," he said. Out of the corner of his eye he saw a black shape advancing toward the open door.

"Well, you'd better get along then," she said. "Or you'll be late."

Reluctantly Pete moved down the walk, toward the street.

He got to school well after the last bell had rung, and he ran down the empty hallways past the posters the third graders had made for the runathon: KEEP MOVING—KEEP HEALTHY. YOUR HEART LOVES YOU WHEN YOU RUN RUN RUN. Out of breath, he opened his classroom door and closed it quickly behind him.

"You're late," said Wanda. "We're almost finished with our workout."

"Good morning, Pete," Miss Patch called out.

She was lying on the floor with her hands folded over her stomach and her feet in the air. The worn soles of her old tennis shoes stuck up over the top of her desk. One of her shoelaces, broken and knotted, was hanging down.

Every morning Miss Patch started the school

day with a workout. First she led the class through the warm-up exercises. Then there were a few minutes of running in place, and after that they walked around slowly, to cool down. Then they did a few stretch exercises and ended with a few moments of relaxation.

"Good morning," Pete mumbled and went quickly to his desk.

"Everybody on their backs on the floor. Pronto!" Miss Patch called out.

There was the usual scramble. Chair legs scraped the floor, books fell and were pushed aside, bodies plunked down.

"Feet in the air," shouted Miss Patch over the hubbub.

Pete stuck his feet up, leaned them against his chair back, and tried not to think about Mishmash.

"When you breathe in, make your stomach go out," the voice coming from under the teacher's desk was reminding them. "When you breathe out, make your stomach go in."

Pete listened to the snuffling and grunting as

everybody pushed their stomachs in and out. He wondered whether Mishmash was still back in his neighborhood rummaging through the garbage cans.

"Close your eyes," called Miss Patch. "Keep breathing."

Pete cast a quick look at Wanda. She was lying there with her nose in the air, her stomach pumping up and down, and her eyes wide open. It would be relaxing just not to have to look at her, thought Pete as he closed his eyes. He decided he had enough to worry about without worrying about Mishmash.

Pete was just drifting off into a pleasant dream about winning the runathon when he felt a poke at his side.

"Quit it," he muttered.

"Look." Wanda's voice grated hoarsely against his ear.

Pete barely lifted his eyelids. He saw a face looking in through the classroom-door window. A familiar face. He opened his eyes wide.

Mishmash!

Pete raised his head and frowned at the face in the window. Mishmash wasn't supposed to be at school. Miss Patch never let him come into the school building.

Mishmash's head was turning slowly. He looked right past Pete's face. His head kept moving until his eyes rested on the teacher's desk.

Mishmash blinked. His nose pressed sideways against the glass. His fat jowls commenced to quiver. Suddenly the dog's head snapped back and his mouth stretched wide.

Mishmash was laughing, thought Pete. He was standing on his hind legs outside Miss Patch's door, looking through the window at the teacher's feet sticking up in the air — and laughing.

Wanda giggled.

"Hands up." The teacher's voice burst upon the quiet of the room. Her hands appeared, extending straight up with fingers spread.

Hands shot up from all over.

"Now shake," she shouted, and began to shake her hands wildly in the air.

Pete saw Mishmash flapping his eyelids in surprise at the room filled with shaking fingers.

"Knees on your chest," Miss Patch cried out as her legs disappeared behind her desk. "Roll over to your side — and stand up."

Her head rose above the top of her desk just as Mishmash's dropped down below the window frame. Miss Patch faced the class, pulling her baggy sweater straight over her wrinkled jeans. A dust ball was sticking to the back of her head.

Everybody popped up like frogs in a pond. Everybody but Harry Hamilton, that is. He had fallen asleep with his feet propped up against his desk top and his hands on his stomach.

———

"I have Mishmash on a new diet," Miss Patch told Pete while everyone but Harry was pushing chairs back into place. "It's especially for over-weight dogs. It has twenty percent fewer calories and less fat." She winked. "All we have to do is make sure he doesn't nibble between meals."

She propped open the door for the bathroom break.

Pete took a quick look out. "Sure," he said with a smile. Mishmash was nowhere to be seen.

Harry woke up and went out, and Pete heard the bang of his locker door. Harry always grabbed a snack secretly during bathroom breaks.

"Hey! Who took my candy bar? Someone took my candy bar!" Harry yelled. He burst into the room, his face red with indignation.

Wanda's mouth began to open. Pete poked her hard.

"Now you shut up. You hear me?" he whispered loudly into her ear. "You just shut up!"

Miss Patch came back into the room and clapped her hands. "Captains! You have five minutes to confer with your teams, and then we'll get on with our work."

"Practice workout right after school," Pete said firmly as his team obediently huddled around him.

"Not me," said Jules. "I don't need to. I work out by myself every day."

"I can't tonight," said Sara. "I have to go to the library."

"Well, if Jules's not coming, I don't see why I have to," said Adele.

"What I want to know is which one of you took my candy bar," said Harry, glowering at them all.

"Time's up!" shouted Miss Patch. She lifted the whistle hanging on a string around her neck, and blew.

Pete slid into his seat, but not before he picked up a paper that had drifted off Wanda's desk.

It was the outline of a big foot.

4

"*One,* two-three-four" Wanda was shouting loudly, like an army sergeant in an old TV movie. Pete noted that she was doing her push ups in front of her house, where she wouldn't miss anything.

He grinned.

It was plain that she hadn't been able to get her team together for an after-school practice workout either.

"*One, two-three-four.*" Wanda's voice raised a notch more as Pete jogged up his walk.

"Pete?" his mother called from the other room as he entered the house. "Take out the garbage, will you?"

"In a minute," Pete shouted back. He bounded

up the stairs and into his bedroom. Hastily clearing the books off his desk, he set out his felt pens and a ruler, and pulled a sheet of notepaper from his folder.

He printed HEALTHY HEART RUNATHON across the top in neat red letters. Carefully he wrote the names of his team members in a trim column on the left side of the page. Taking up his black pen and the ruler, he drew, under each name, firm lines extending all the way across the page. Then he divided each row into squares by drawing lines up and down from top to bottom.

Pete sat back to look at his work. He approved the straightness of the lines and the orderly lettering. He was good at making charts. He was good at graphs and maps and diagrams. He liked figuring and measuring and planning and organizing. He liked working with numbers. Arithmetic was his favorite subject.

As a final touch, he retraced the *J* in Jules's name at the bottom of the list, and then sat back to admire his handiwork.

For every half-mile lap around the school field, he would color in a square with his red felt marker. At the end of the runathon, the added-up squares divided by two would total the miles.

Pete put the chart back into his folder, went downstairs, and started to do push ups. He went from push ups to crab walks. He was getting pretty good at crab-walking. Arching his stomach and walking backward on his hands and feet, he scurried all the way across the living-room floor and into the kitchen before he sprawled.

"When you pick yourself up, you can take out the garbage," his mother reminded him.

Pete hauled the full sack of garbage outside. He dumped it into the can behind the garage just as his father drove up. Pete crab-walked across the yard. His father was kneeling in front of the radish patch.

"Well, how do they look?" Pete's mother said as she came out to greet him.

"Ready for thinning," Mr. Peters reported happily.

Pete got to his feet and brushed the dirt off his knees. He went to look. Rows of small green plants filled the plot.

"I can almost taste them already," said Mr. Peters. "There's nothing so crisp and fresh as young radishes right out of the garden."

Pete dropped down to the ground again to do some more push ups.

His father stopped inspecting his radishes to watch Pete for a moment. "Don't you think you're taking this runathon business a little too seriously?" he inquired gravely.

"Pete takes everything seriously," his mother answered for him. She laughed. "He has a one-track mind. Just like his father."

"Everyone's taking the Healthy Heart Runathon seriously," Pete said. "Even the principal." He didn't go on to tell them that there were posters in the hallways and green and yellow and blue and red teams in every room, because his father's nose was pointed down into the radish patch again and his mother had turned to poke at her First Lady rosebush.

"I think I'll go for a practice run," he said instead, and jogged out of the yard.

Pete felt good running. He began to take deep breaths. He smelled grass growing and Scotch broom blooming and dinners beginning to cook. He heard kids yelling and TVs blaring.

He was enjoying himself so much that he ran right past Miss Patch's house before he noticed where he was. He turned back and jogged through her gate and up to the front porch.

"How's Mishmash?" he said breathlessly when the teacher opened her door. He kept his feet going in place on the doormat.

Miss Patch didn't seem to notice that Pete was bobbing up and down in front of her.

"You know what I caught him doing when I got home from school today?" she said.

Automatically Pete's feet stopped moving. "What?"

"Stuffing chocolate eclairs into his mouth," she said.

"Chocolate eclairs? Where did he get the chocolate eclairs?"

"Out of the top of Mrs. Tribble's grocery bag, that's where." Miss Patch jerked her head toward the house next door. "It was sitting on her porch while she unlocked her door."

"Oh," said Pete and turned to look at the house next door. The shades were all down tight. Mrs. Tribble always pulled her shades down when she was good and mad.

"I had to go right out and buy her some more," Miss Patch said, and she sounded pretty mad herself.

There was a thump, and Mishmash's head pushed around the corner of the door. The black eyes gazed at Pete. The face began to grin.

Pete glared at the dog. "You'd better shape up, Mishmash. You've got to stop snitching. You hear me?" He stuck his face close to the dog's ear.

"You're getting way too fat!"

Mishmash's grin disappeared. He backed away, into the house. He must have given the door a push, because it slammed, forcing Miss Patch out onto her porch.

Pete heard her vigorously knocking at her front door as he went out the gate and headed toward home and dinner. He turned his attention back to running. Sara passed him, riding her bike and reading a book at the same time. To set a good example, he swung his arms and lifted his knees high. He went past Jules Ivar's house without changing pace.

"Hey! Wait up!" Jules came out his door and sprinted to catch up with Pete. His T-shirt had red numbers printed on it. His running shoes were professional. His head, bobbing along, reached no higher than Pete's shoulder.

"You're lifting your knees too high," Jules said loudly.

Pete lurched. "What?"

"Your knees. You're lifting them too high. You tire the leg muscles when you lift them high."

Pete looked down at his knees.

Jules ran backward, talking all the while. "Think of your knees as pistons. See? You get smoother running if the pistons go up and down short and fast. Pick up your knees just high enough to keep your engine chugging along. Like this." Jules turned and moved ahead.

Pete caught up and chugged along beside him. "Wanda is telling everybody her team is going to win," he said as they went past the school.

Jules laughed. "I'm not worried."

Pete grinned. He wasn't either. Not with Jules on his team.

"I'm small but I'm fast," said Jules.

"You're fast, all right." Pete was beginning to puff a little.

"Well, I'll tell you why," said Jules, talking out of the side of his mouth nearest Pete. He tapped at his forehead. "That's why. I mean, when you're

small like me, you've got to use more than your body. Believe me."

Pete nodded.

"I mean — your size or shape doesn't make much difference if you use your mind."

"How do you mean?"

"To figure ahead," said Jules. "Marathon runners, they've got to use their minds to keep going. They've got to look at the course as if it were an arithmetic problem." He cocked his head toward Pete. "And they've got to come out with the right answer if they're going to finish up front." They had circled the block and were now in front of Jules's house again. Jules tapped his head. "Runners don't need a killer instinct to win, they just need an arithmetic mind," he said as he turned up the walk.

Pete felt a smile coming over his mouth. The one thing he was good at was arithmetic. He chugged the rest of the way home with the smile on his face.

———

Getting out of bed the next morning, Pete began to make low humming sounds like a motor revving. He jumped into his clothes and chugged down the stairs and into the kitchen.

His father was washing his hands at the kitchen sink.

"Harrrrrruuuuuuuummmmmm," Pete murmured as he sat down at the table.

His father turned around. "What did you say?"

"Nothing," said Pete. He went on harrumming to himself. "I didn't say anything."

Mr. Peters sat down across from him and slapped butter onto a slice of toast. "My radishes are flourishing," he announced.

"I found a new recipe for radish relish," said Mrs. Peters.

Pete looked out the window and saw Wanda crossing their back yard. She was wearing a yellow headband around her head, Indian style. Under her arm was her clipboard.

"Who's that?" said Mr. Peters, and put on his glasses.

39

"Wanda," said Pete.

"Wanda?" said Mr. Peters, as if he had never heard of her before.

"You know Wanda," Mrs. Peters replied. "The little girl next door."

"Oh, *that* Wanda." Mr. Peters gazed out the window. "What's she trying to sell now?"

Pete laughed.

His mother looked at both of them severely. "Wanda is undoubtedly still selling pledges for the runathon," she said.

"Runathon? What runathon?" Mr. Peters looked blankly around the table.

"Our Healthy Heart Runathon," Pete reminded. "It starts with spring vacation."

His mother sighed as the front doorbell rang. She arose and went out of the kitchen to answer it. Pete splashed more milk onto his Cheerioats, stirred, shoved a spoonful into his mouth and, in his mind, began running. He ran himself around the school track, his knees going up and down like pistons.

"Well, if persistence is what it takes, Wanda's certainly got it," Pete heard his mother say.

Pete's mind leaped back to the breakfast table. His mother was sitting down again. "What she hasn't got is an arithmetic mind," he said loudly.

Mr. Peters turned his head and stared at his son. "The kids in this neighborhood have all gone crazy," he said, and went back to eating his breakfast.

5

Pete rolled out of bed. He lay down on his rug on the floor to stretch. He wiggled his toes. Then, conscientiously, he rotated his feet at the ankles, both feet at the same time, doing shin-splint preventers. He counted twenty rotations before he sat up.

"It's the first day of the runathon," Wanda reminded Pete when she saw him at the front door of his house later that morning.

Pete reached back to make sure his Healthy

Heart Runathon chart was in his pants pocket, folded and ready. He wasn't going to waste any time talking to Wanda.

She gave him a watchful smile. "I wouldn't depend too much on Jules Ivar," she said helpfully. "He's not the dependable type, if you know what I mean."

Pete made a snorting sound and headed for the school field. The green flag was up when he got there. Later it would be replaced by the yellow flag for Wanda's team and all the other yellows.

Each team had to stick to its special time slot until the last day of the runathon. On the last day any team could run anytime — all day, if it wanted.

Pete saw Adele waiting, swinging on the bars as usual. Harry was sitting cross-legged on the ground eating a candy bar. Sara was lying on her stomach on the bench reading a book. Jules was standing on his head.

Every class had its own meeting place for warm-ups. Pete's team had the area closest to the bars and swings. The first- and second-grade teams were meeting under the porticoes, and the third and fourth graders were warming up in the parking lot.

"Okay, everybody," Pete said. "Let's warm up."

Adele dropped off the monkey bars and came and sat down next to Jules. Harry stretched his legs out and sighed. "I've already warmed up," said Jules, still standing on his head.

"I didn't see you," said Pete. "According to the rules, it doesn't count unless the captain sees you. I'm the captain, and I didn't see you."

"Oh brother," said Sara, slamming her book closed. She came and sat on the ground with the rest of them.

"I saw him," said Adele. She smiled at Jules.

"We have to follow the rules," Pete said.

"Yah. Rules." Harry's cheeks blobbed when he nodded.

Jules flipped to his feet. "Let's get going, then."

"First the shin-splint preventer." Pete stuck out his legs and rotated his feet.

"I never did see what sitting around wiggling

your feet does for you," complained Adele.

"You'd know if you were a professional basket-ball player," said Jules. "Shin splints hurt."

"Second warm up," shouted Pete. "Knee hugs."

Flopping onto her back, Sara brought one knee up to touch her chin.

"Now the other knee," Pete said.

"Owwwwww," Harry groaned. He was pressing his knee against his stomach, but his stomach stuck out too far.

"It's easy!" Jules said. He touched his chin with first one knee, then the other.

Adele threw him an admiring glance. Then she modestly wrapped her skirt around her legs and tried to pull her knee up to reach her chin. "I don't see how you always do it so easily," she said to Jules.

Harry puffed and groaned. Sara jumped up and leaned forward with one knee bent and the other leg straight out behind her.

"The Achilles' tendon stretch," announced Pete, doing the same.

"That hurts," said Harry.

"It's supposed to hurt, dummy," said Sara.

Hastily Pete said, "Okay, Sara. You go first. Then Adele, then Jules, then Harry, then me."

"I think Jules should go first," Adele said. "Because he's the fastest runner."

"It doesn't make any difference who goes first," said Jules, hopping up to the front of the line anyway. "We're not racing. We're just running."

"I'm not," said Harry, dropping in behind Adele. "I'm not running at all. I'm just going to walk."

"Oh brother," said Sara. She started jogging along the narrow path at the edge of the playground.

"It's not supposed to make any difference whether you walk or run or jog," Pete reminded them. "Just so you cover laps. Once around is one-half mile. Twice around is one mile. Do as many laps as you can, and meet back at the bars so I can mark the chart."

"I'm finished right now," Harry gasped, and stopped running. His cheeks were red, and his breath came out in little puffs.

"No you're not!" said Jules, who had already run around the track once and come up behind them. He jabbed Harry's behind.

"You cut that out!"

"Let's go!" shouted Pete. He ran smartly, passing Harry by, passing Adele, and running along beside Sara until she dropped back to a walk. Jules was already halfway around the track again.

Twenty minutes later the team members had all straggled back to the starting place.

"Don't sit down!" hollered Jules. "You have to cool down first."

They all kept moving slowly for a minute or two and then flopped onto the ground.

"Boy am I hungry!" said Harry.

"After the cooldown, we do stretch exercises," Pete reminded everybody.

Harry groaned. Sara muttered. Adele pretended

she couldn't do all those things because she was wearing a skirt. Finally, all arching up with stomachs to the sky, they crab-walked to the bench, Harry puffing and blowing. Then, for the relaxation windup, they flopped flat on their backs with their legs propped against the bench and their hands on their stomachs.

"Next time I'm going to bring some doughnuts," said Harry. "I sure wish I had a doughnut."

"I brought a cookie," said Adele. She smiled. Not at Harry. At Jules.

"No cookies, no doughnuts," Pete said firmly. "Not until we enter our laps on the chart." He unrolled the score chart, laid it on the bench, and took his red felt pen out of his jeans pocket. Carefully he blocked in a half-mile square next to Harry's name.

"Don't forget mine," said Adele.

Pete filled in the square next to Adele's name, keeping within the lines, making each stroke of the felt pen very firm and sure.

"Altogether we must have covered ten miles to-day," said Jules.

Pete started filling out the square next to Sara's name. "We have to do more than ten miles tomorrow — if we want to stay ahead of Wanda."

"We're a cinch." Jules snapped his fingers and stood on his head as Pete slowly and carefully inked in some more squares.

"Where'd that big fat dog come from?" he heard Adele say.

Pete looked up. Mishmash stood at the edge of the school grounds, surveying the area with interest. Pete frowned.

"Isn't that Miss Patch's dog?" Jules asked. He was frowning too. He didn't like dogs. He particularly didn't like big dogs like Mishmash.

Adele sniffed. "He's not supposed to be here."

"Go home," hollered Harry and tossed a pebble. He wasn't very good at throwing. The pebble hit the ground several feet in front of the dog. Mishmash walked up and sniffed at it.

"Go home, Mishmash!" Pete made his voice extra loud and stern.

Mishmash looked a little surprised.

"Home!" ordered Pete. He stretched out his arm and pointed in the direction of the teacher's house.

Mishmash moved a step or two backward.

"Don't forget to record my laps," said Jules.

"I'm doing it." Pete devoted all his attention to filling in the squares in the bottom row next to Jules's name.

Jules flung his head back, placed a little bear-shaped jug to his mouth, and squeezed a stream of honey down his throat.

"What's that for?" Harry asked. His mouth worked as if he were tasting the honey too.

Jules licked a drop off his lips and replaced the cap. "Energy restorer." He stuck the little plastic bottle into his back pocket.

"Want half my cookie?" Adele held it out invitingly. "It's got chocolate chips."

"No thanks," said Jules.

"Whifff," said Mishmash, who had sneaked up close to the group.

"Mishmash!" Pete shouted warningly. But not soon enough.

Mishmash's mouth snapped open. He gulped and blinked.

"My cookie!" screeched Adele. "He grabbed my cookie!"

"He probably thought you were offering it to him," said Pete, and glared at Mishmash.

"Dogs don't think," Adele said with a sniff.

Mishmash raised his head, regarded Adele, and gave a little sniff of his own.

"It was just an accident," Pete said, loudly, because he was sure it wasn't.

6

Miss Patch was defrosting her refrigerator. Her sweater was buttoned wrong. The hem of her skirt was coming down, and one sock had slid off her heel and into her shoe.

"Do you know what he's eaten since yesterday?" She didn't wait for Pete to answer.

"He's consumed a rhubarb pie, a peanut-butter sandwich, six cupcakes, four bananas, two candy bars, half a chicken, a package of bologna, three apples, a waffle, and the plastic rose on my bedside table."

"He ate a plastic rose?"

"It was pink," said Miss Patch.

Pete decided not to mention that he'd also eaten Adele's cookie the day before. He sighed. The scolding he had given Mishmash hadn't done much good.

"All he does is eat," said Miss Patch. "He eats everything!" She waved at the kitchen-cabinet doors, which were hanging open. The only cupboard closed was the one under the sink, where Miss Patch kept the special diet dog food.

"Except his diet food," she added grimly.

Pete went out on Miss Patch's porch and sat down next to Mishmash. He frowned at the dog, who was lying on the upside-down welcome mat with his eyes closed.

"Mishmash?" Pete said loudly.

The dog began to snore.

The gate opened and Wanda came up the walk in a new pair of yellow running shorts, her headband, and her mother's green-rimmed sunglasses. She was slurping at a soft-drink bottle.

Pete looked at her calculatingly. "How many

miles did your team run yesterday? Six? Ten? Twenty?" He grinned. One thing he was sure of. No one could beat Jules.

Wanda wiped her mouth with the back of her arm. She smiled. "How's Mishmash?"

Pete didn't even bother to answer.

"Want some?" She pushed the bottle neck under his nose.

He jerked his head back. "No thanks."

Wanda shrugged. "It's only diet pop." She took a long gulp and grimaced as she wiped her mouth with the back of her hand. "Our whole freezer is full of nothing but diet food. If you're not on a diet in our house, you'd starve."

"There's someone around here who's not much interested in diet food," said Pete. He stared at Mishmash. "There's someone around here who couldn't care less about diet food —"

Miss Patch's voice came through the open front door, interrupting Pete. "There's someone around here who'd better change his ways or he's going to find the cupboards bare of even diet food."

The big hairy blob on the doormat opened an eye, burped, and closed it again.

Miss Patch came out the door trying to stick her arm, which had a purse hanging from it, into a sweater. She stepped over Mishmash and went down the walk and through the gate.

"Don't let him eat anything!" she shouted back at them as she let the gate slam shut.

Pete stared glumly at the holes in the front lawn. So far as he could see, that was an impossible assignment.

Wanda took another gulp of her diet drink. "The trouble is that he's a compulsive eater," she said. "When you're a compulsive eater, you have to eat all the time. My mother has a friend whose little boy is a compulsive eater. He'll eat anything."

"Nobody eats just anything," said Pete, because he felt like arguing. Whenever he talked to Wanda he felt like arguing.

"This kid does," said Wanda. "He'll eat food out of a dog dish, stale bread thrown out for the birds — anything. He doesn't care what it is. Rotten apples, sticks of butter, sour milk . . ."

Pete suddenly remembered the teacher's empty cupboards.

"Once this kid went to a bake sale and ate three pies," Wanda said.

"What kind of pies?"

Wanda gave Pete a pitying look. "What difference does it make what kind of pies?" she said. "When you turn into a compulsive eater, you'll eat any kind, whether you like them or not. My mother says that if they don't watch him he's likely to eat himself to death."

Pete stood up. "You shut up!" he hollered. "You understand me? You just shut up!"

Wanda gazed at him a moment, then lifted her bottle and took a long slow drink. Pete could hear the liquid gurgling down her throat. He heard the unpleasant sucking sound of her lips as they let go of the bottle top.

"Of course, if worse comes to worst, we could try hypnosis," suggested Wanda helpfully. "Hypnosis is used all the time to help people cure themselves of overeating and smoking and insomnia." She glanced at Pete. "That's what you have when you can't sleep."

"I know what it is!" Pete yelled. "And whatever it is, Mishmash doesn't have it!"

Wanda poked at the animal. "Wake up, Fatso."

Pete glowered at her. "His name is Mishmash."

"His name," said Wanda, "is plain Blubber, no matter what you call him."

Pete heard himself shouting again. "He can't help it if he has a healthy appetite!"

Wanda smiled.

"It's not going to work," Pete said as he watched Wanda take off her ring and tie a piece of string to it.

"We won't know," said Wanda, "until we try. Anyway, this is just to focus his attention." She swung the ring around in the air.

Mishmash sat up. Wanda began swinging the ring in front of his face. Mishmash blinked.

"Watch it closely, Mishmash," said Wanda.

Mishmash's eyes moved from side to side as he followed the swing of the shiny object on the end of the string.

"Watch the pretty ring," Wanda said in a sing-song voice. "Watch it swing. Watch it shine. See how shiny it is. Back and forth. Back and forth."

"Whfff," said Mishmash, moving his head from side to side as the ring swung.

"And now you are getting very tired," said Wanda slowly. "Very very tired. Your eyelids are getting heavier and heavier. Your eyelids are closing."

Mishmash's eyes closed, opened again, closed. He turned his back on the ring, turned all the way around, sat down on the porch, settled his jaw on his paw, and began to snore.

Pete laughed. "See? It didn't work."

Wanda paid no attention to Pete. "Mishmash?" she said.

The dog lifted his tail and let it fall with a thump.

"Sure it's working," said Wanda. "I put him to sleep, didn't I?"

Pete gave her a pitying glance. "You didn't put him to sleep. All you did is wake him up. And he went back to sleep by himself."

Wanda untied the ring and put it back on her finger. "Well, he took my suggestion. That's all hypnosis is. Suggestion."

Pete laughed.

"Quiet!" Wanda said. Then very softly she said, "Mishmash?"

The dog's eyelids quivered — and stayed closed.

"Listen to me, Mishmash. And listen carefully. In a minute I'm going to wake you up. And when I say 'Wake up,' what you'll be hungry for is diet food. Not chocolate eclairs, not pie, not bread. Not even fried chicken. When I count one, two, three, and say 'Open your eyes,' you won't feel hungry for chocolate eclairs and pies and bread and fried chicken. So in a few seconds' time, I'm counting one two three and saying 'Open your eyes,' and you will open your eyes and you won't feel hungry — except for diet food. Now — one, two, three. Open your eyes."

They both stared at the dog. Mishmash's eyelids quivered.

"Wake up, Mishmash!" said Pete loudly.

The dog opened his mouth and yawned. One eye came open, and then the other.

Wanda smiled. "Good dog," she said, patting his head.

Mishmash stood up and shook himself. He grinned at her.

Wanda hastily stepped back, knocking over the bottle of soda behind her. Pete watched it roll off the step and spill onto the walk.

Mishmash watched it too. He waddled across the porch and down the steps, stopped a moment to lick at the mouth of the diet-drink bottle, and moved off around the house.

Wanda went to pick up the bottle. She gave Pete a knowing smile.

Pete laughed. He laughed so hard he almost fell to the ground laughing.

"What's so funny?" Wanda said.

"You don't really think you hypnotized him, do you?"

Wanda looked thoughtfully at the ring she had replaced on her finger. "Well, I agree; it's pretty unusual to hypnotize a dog." She carried the bottle down to the gate. She opened the gate, turned around, and looked triumphantly back at Pete. "But then, as you're always saying, Mishmash is a pretty unusual dog." She snapped the gate closed behind her.

7

Pete went home.

When he got there, his father was inspecting the radish patch. "They're almost ready to pick," his father said. He sounded happy.

Because his father seemed to expect him to, Pete went to look. All he saw were green leaves on stalks a few inches high. He didn't see any radishes.

"They're underground," his father said. Mr. Peters knelt down and gently pulled at a cluster of leaves growing above the soil. A round red globe came out, trailed by a thin white thread of a root.

"Beautiful," said Pete's mother when his father brought it into the house.

Holding the radish as if it were a large pearl, Mr. Peters tenderly rinsed it under the water faucet, sprinkled it with salt, and popped it into his mouth. There was a crisp crunch as his teeth bit into it.

"Ahhhhh!" he said. "There's nothing that tastes quite as good as a radish plucked from your own garden."

"Are they ready?" Mrs. Peters asked as she picked up a bowl.

Mr. Peters chewed thoughtfully and looked at the ceiling. "Let's give them another day," he said. "Another day and they should be at their very peak."

It was time for the green teams to begin their warm ups, so Pete headed for school. His team was waiting for him at the usual place. Adele was on the bars. Sara, reading a book, was straddling the bench. Harry lay on his back munching an apple.

"Where's Jules?" Pete asked.

Sara looked up. "He's not coming." She turned a page.

Adele stopped swinging. Harry sat up.

"How do you know?" said Adele.

"Because I was there when his mother phoned to say good-by to my mother. They've gone to Arizona to his grandmother's funeral. They won't be back until the end of spring vacation."

Pete felt his breakfast lurch in his stomach.

"You mean we have to be in the runathon without him?" shrieked Adele.

"His mother called the principal and told him we'd have to find a replacement," Sara reported.

"Who?" said Pete. He had trouble getting the word out of his tight throat. Everyone in Miss Patch's class was already part of a team group.

Sara shrugged. "That's your job. You're the captain."

"Well, there goes the ball game," muttered Harry.

"You mean we don't have to run anymore if we don't want to?" Adele was rising from the bench as if she were already on her way home.

"Shut up," said Harry.

With a disappointed expression, Adele sat down again.

Everyone was quiet, waiting.

Pete looked around at his teammates: Sara, with her book; Harry, who had never been any good at anything; and Adele, who hated to run and did her laps mostly walking instead. He thought of Wanda. Wanda would take it as a personal triumph if his team fell apart.

Pete pressed his lips together. He wasn't going to let it fall apart. "I'll think of someone," he said.

————

"Too bad you lost your best runner," Wanda said with a smirk when Pete reached home.

"Who said he was our best runner?" Pete said, scowling at her.

"Anyone who knows anything at all about running knows that Jules was your best," she said. "You won't ever find anyone as good to take his place."

"What makes you think I won't?" Pete said loudly.

Wanda grinned. "Because Jules was worth twice as much as anyone else on your team. You're going to have to find someone with four legs to match him." She laughed.

"Is that a fact?"

"The fact is — seeing as you're always so careful about facts — he was probably almost as good as I am," Wanda said.

Pete smiled. A long slow smile. "To be absolutely accurate, I seem to remember that dealing with facts is not exactly your strong point. As a matter of fact, if I might say so, anything that has to do with facts is your worst subject."

Pete felt more than pleased at the sour expression that had come over Wanda's face.

"You're out of your mind," she said.

For a moment or two, Pete had the glorious satisfaction of feeling superior to Wanda.

"By the way, I think you ought to know —" she began.

He waited. Then, in spite of himself, he heard himself say, "What?"

"We just had a burglar-alarm system put into our house."

"So?"

"So it might be a smart idea if you let Mishmash know what he's up against."

Pete snorted. "What makes you think your burglar alarm would have anything to do with Mishmash?"

Wanda raised her eyebrows. "If you were half as smart as you think you are, you'd know that our burglar alarm has everything to do with Mishmash."

"What do you mean by that?" shouted Pete. But he didn't need an answer from Wanda. He already knew.

"My mother won't have to worry about anyone walking into her house anymore," Wanda said. "When the burglar alarm is on, no one can open a door or a window without tripping the alarm."

Pete gazed at the Sparlings' house. Mrs. Sparling was just coming around the corner with her garden gloves on, hurrying as if she heard the telephone ringing. Pete saw her rush up the front steps, put her hand on the door, and push it open.

Brrrrrrrrrrrinnnng! Pete jumped at the sound. It tore through the neighborhood.

Mrs. Barnes stuck her head out of an upstairs window from across the street. "Someone call the police!" she shouted.

The bell stopped just as suddenly as it had begun.

"What happened?" Mrs. Anderson, who had come out of her house, asked.

"Did they catch him?" screamed Mrs. Berty, running up the street toward them.

"Catch who?" said Pete.

"The burglar, that's who," said Mrs. Anderson.

Wanda poked Pete with her elbow.

"I didn't see any burglar," said Pete.

A police car came up the street. It stopped in front of Wanda's house, and two officers got out. One sped around to the back of the house. The other walked quickly to the front door.

Mrs. Sparling came out, walking rather stiffly.

She spoke to the officer, and then he went back to his car and got in and honked for his partner.

Wanda began to giggle. "False alarm."

"Oh for heaven's sake!" said Mrs. Barnes, and banged the window shut.

Mrs. Anderson went back into her house.

———

"The Sparlings' new burglar alarm has gone off by mistake three times today," Mrs. Peters told Mr. Peters when he arrived home later.

"Is that so?" said Mr. Peters, as if it didn't make much difference to him.

Mrs. Peters sighed. "This used to be such a nice quiet neighborhood," she said. "When we first moved here, no one thought of keeping their doors locked in broad daylight."

"Times are changing all over," said Mr. Peters.

Pete remembered that Mishmash had come to live with his family shortly after they had moved into the neighborhood. It was never very quiet again after Mishmash moved in with them, Pete recalled. He decided not to mention that.

"What are we having for dinner?" he said, to change the subject.

"Radishes, for one thing. That is, if they're ready to harvest." Mrs. Peters looked at Mr. Peters.

Mr. Peters smiled. He took a big bowl out of the cupboard. "I'd say the time is just about exactly right. I'd say those radishes should be at the very peak of perfection." He was halfway out the door. "You want to come and help me pick?" he called back to Pete.

"No thanks," said Pete. He slumped into a chair. He had enough to do, without digging up radishes. He had to find a replacement for Jules. And he had to figure out what to do about Mishmash before Miss Patch . . .

A howl arose from the garden. Pete jumped. His mother dropped a plate.

"For heaven's sake!" she said, and ran to the kitchen door. Hastily Pete followed.

Pete's father was standing there with the bowl in his hands. It was empty.

"What's the matter?" Mrs. Peters shrieked.

"Someone stole my radishes! That's what's the matter," he yelled.

Pete gazed at the torn-up patch of earth. Only a few radishes remained — pulled up, stepped on, mangled. Their tops were chewed, their roots broken.

"I wonder who could have done it," Mrs. Peters gasped.

Feeling a little sick, Pete went back into the house. He didn't have to wonder. He knew.

8

That night Pete lay in his bed staring at the ceiling. After a while he flopped over and closed his eyes. But his mind wouldn't go to sleep. His thoughts leaped around like grasshoppers. He rolled over. But no matter how he turned, he could find no answer to either of his problems. He couldn't replace Jules, and he couldn't keep Mishmash from overeating. He could think of no way to bring Jules back or to make Mishmash lose weight.

Pete pushed his face into the pillow. Even with his eyes closed he could see the wreckage of his father's radish patch.

He must have fallen asleep, because he woke suddenly out of a dream in which he was running with his knees going up too high and Mishmash barking at him.

He wondered what had awakened him. It was still pretty dark. He raised his head and peered toward the open window. An airplane hummed high over the house. A breeze rattled a paper on his desk. Pete sat up. A solution had blown into his mind. A solution so simple that he wondered why he hadn't thought of it before.

———

When Pete reached the school ground the next morning, the three members of his team were sitting on the ground together waiting. Paper sacks full of the usual peanut-butter sandwiches and chocolate-chip cookies, as well as Harry's ration of candy bars, formed a lineup on the bench.

Pete came striding toward them with Mishmash lumbering behind him. Harry rolled over to his side and pushed himself up off the ground when he saw them coming.

"You didn't find anybody," Harry said by way of greeting, and he looked disappointed.

"Sure I did," said Pete.

"When's he coming?"

"He's here."

"Here?" Adele looked all around.

Sara's face took on an expression of disbelief. "That dog. You don't mean that dog!"

"That's who I mean," said Pete. "Mishmash. He's our new team member."

"Oh brother!" Sara sat down on the grass and covered her eyes with her hands.

"Who ever heard of a dog being in a runathon?" Adele said, sniffing.

Mishmash began edging over toward the lunch sacks on the bench. Pete grabbed him by the collar.

"He doesn't look like much of a runner to me," said Adele. "He's too fat."

"According to the rules, we're not supposed to make any personal remarks about fellow team members," Harry said in a self-righteous tone.

"I think the only case in point," said Sara, "is what kind of a team member he'll be."

Adele sniffed. "Well, if he can't run as well as Jules I don't think it's going to matter what kind of a member he is."

Sara said, "I have to admit it would be very unusual for anyone to run as well as Jules."

Pete smiled. "Mishmash is a very unusual dog."

Everyone turned and looked at Mishmash doubtfully. Mishmash closed his eyes and yawned.

"The least we can do is give him a tryout," suggested Harry.

"You mean I have to run with a dog?" Adele shrieked.

"Well, the dog has to run with you," Sara pointed out.

Adele's glance flitted from one team member to another. No one said anything. She gave a little laugh, shook the hair out of her eyes, and said, "Well, I guess it's okay by me. I'm certainly not going to be the one to tell on you."

Harry shrugged. "Live and let live, that's my motto."

Pete focused his eyes on Sara. There was a glint in her eyes. No mistaking it. A glint of admiration. He pretended he didn't see it. "Okay! Let's get going."

Mishmash stood around sleepily staring at the four of them as they began the warm-up exercises.

"Come on, Mishmash," Pete said. "You have to warm up too."

The dog lowered his bulging belly to the ground, spread out his legs, and looked curiously at the others. Obligingly, he rolled over when they lay on their backs and hugged their knees.

"He's stepping on me," Adele complained. "Get off my foot, you blimp!" she yelled at the dog.

"No personal remarks!" reminded Harry.

Mishmash ambled aimlessly after them as they started down the track. He lumbered along well behind the others all the way around. "Come on boy," Pete kept calling as he turned around every few steps. But it didn't do much good. Mishmash

just sat down where he was and rested until they all came around a second time. He blinked at them without showing much interest in the cooldown, and got in everybody's way during the stretch exercises.

"Boy, I'm getting hungry," said Harry.

"First the crab walk," Pete reminded. "Then a little relaxation, and then we'll all eat."

Everybody did the crab walk. Even Mishmash tried it. And as they flopped onto their backs for five minutes of relaxing, Mishmash kept right on walking.

Pete wasn't too pleased with the morning's workout. He unrolled the chart and marked the correct number of laps next to each name. He crossed out Jules's name and below it printed in bold letters the name MISHMASH.

Pete raised his head. "Mishmash?" He looked around.

"My lunch!" Adele shrieked. "He took my lunch!"

Pete whirled around. Mishmash was in the midst of a scatter of empty lunch sacks. Startled by Adele's scream, he stood there with a piece of celery hanging out of his mouth.

As they all ran toward him shouting, Mishmash darted away. He raced around the whole track twice before they could catch up with him.

"Oh brother!" Sara said as she flopped down on the ground. Her hair hung over her face. The bottom of her T-shirt was sticking out of her shorts.

Harry, puffing and bellowing, flopped down beside her. He had run all the way around the track without stopping.

"I told you!" Adele screamed. "I told you it wouldn't work!"

Pete plopped down beside her. He was breathing hard, but he was smiling. "What d'you mean it doesn't work? Sure it works. He did as many laps as Jules, didn't he?"

Harry raised his sweating red face. "And for the first time, *we* all did too!"

9

The sound of Mrs. Sparling's burglar alarm jangled Pete awake. He sat up in bed. A slit of light appeared under his bedroom door. He heard the creak of his parents' bed and the sound of his father's bare feet slapping across the floor to the window. The ringing stopped.

Pete eased down into bed again and fell asleep.

Mr. Peters's face wore a pained expression when he came downstairs for breakfast the next morning. "The Sparlings' bell went off again," he said. "In the middle of the night."

"It was probably just another false alarm," Mrs.

Peters said. She yawned too as she poured two cups of coffee.

Pete began to eat his cereal.

Wanda's face appeared in the window of the kitchen door. "Did you hear about the burglar?" she said eagerly as she came in.

"What burglar?" said Pete.

"The one who got into our basement last night."

Mrs. Peters put her coffee cup down. Pete stopped eating.

Wanda stood in the middle of their kitchen acting important. She rolled her eyes. "You should see our basement. Everything in the freezer tossed out."

A small persistent thudding began in Pete's chest. "What was he looking for?"

"I don't know what he was looking for, but I know what he got."

"What?" the Peters family said all together.

"All my mother's Weight Watchers frozen dinners," she said.

Mrs. Peters laughed. "What kind of a burglar

would want to steal nothing but frozen dinners?"

"The same kind that would steal radishes," suggested Mr. Peters grimly.

"He could have been on a strict diet, I suppose," said Wanda.

"Who ever heard of a fat burglar?" said Mrs. Peters.

"Veal Parmigiana," said Wanda. "Turkey Tetrazzini. Chile Con Carne. Veal Sausage Pizza Pie. Lasagna with Cheese, Veal, and Sauce . . ."

"Oh my!" said Mrs. Peters.

"That's not what my mother said." Wanda grimaced. "She was pretty upset. My father wasn't, though. He doesn't like diet dinners anyway. He complains all the time about having to eat diet food just because my mother has to."

"Well, I think that anyone who steals someone else's food is nothing more than an animal," said Mrs. Peters.

Pete put down his spoon.

———

Outside, Wanda poked at him. "It finally worked," she said in a loud whisper.

"What worked?"

"My hypnotism, of course." She had a smug look on her face. "He's eating diet food. Just like I told him to." Then she frowned. "But I didn't expect him to go so far as to steal it."

Pete laughed. He made so much noise laughing that Mrs. Sparling stuck her head out the door.

"You're lucky she didn't stuff a can of tuna fish down your throat," said Wanda after her mother closed the door.

Pete stared at what was left of the radishes. Mishmash had dug up his father's radish patch. He was sure of that. Could he have stolen Mrs. Sparling's Weight Watchers dinners too?

"How do you know it was Mishmash?" he said loudly, to cover his own suspicion.

Wanda flipped her hair out of her eyes. "All you have to do is know Mishmash."

"It could have been someone else," said Pete, trying to sound positive.

"Who? Just tell me who?"

"It could have been anyone," said Pete, almost believing it. "Probably someone you'd least suspect."

Wanda's father came out of her house. He walked with a spring in his step. There was a large smile on his face. They watched as he got into his car and backed it out of the driveway.

Wanda turned to stare after her father's car as it disappeared down the driveway.

Pete began to grin.

"That's ridiculous!" Wanda shouted after Pete as he jogged away down the street.

Miss Patch met him at her front door, her teeth sticking out in a happy smile. "Mishmash is watching television," she said. "But he hasn't tried to sneak into the refrigerator today. Not even once."

Pete thought of the empty freezer at Wanda's house and didn't feel surprised that Mishmash wasn't very hungry.

"Come on, Mishmash," he said, and dragged the dog out to the front yard.

He tied a piece of clothesline to the dog's collar and pulled him almost all the way to the schoolground.

At school, Pete led his team through the warm up. Mishmash moved around among them as they did the exercises. When they sat down, he sat down; when they rolled over, he rolled over. It was plain to see that he was beginning to enjoy the warm up.

"He keeps sticking his paws in my face," Adele complained.

"He's just trying to do what you do," said Pete.

"When someone tries to do what you do, that's a compliment," said Sara. She stood up after her knee hugs, and began to shake the grass clippings off her jacket.

Mishmash scrambled up and gave himself a shake.

"He's a fat nuisance," Adele said as she moved away from the dog.

"Well, just keep him running around the track and he'll slim down some. Like me," Harry said proudly.

Pete stared at Harry. Was it his imagination, or did Harry's face seem less fat, and his belly not quite so soft?

"Do you think Mishmash is slimming down some?" he asked hopefully.

"He doesn't look so fat to me anymore," Sara said.

"That's just because we're getting used to seeing him fat," Adele said. "When you see someone around a lot, you get used to their being fat. You hardly notice it."

"Well, I notice it on Mishmash," Pete said. "I notice it a lot."

Mishmash raised his head and grinned at Pete.

"You're too fat, Mishmash," Pete said. "You hear me? You're too fat!"

"You shouldn't be scolding him all the time," Harry said. "Every time my Aunt Grace comes over, she keeps telling me to watch my weight.

'Watch your weight, watch your weight,' " Harry said in a high voice. "She makes me so nervous, I eat twice as much as usual. I gobble up everything in sight."

But Pete wasn't paying much attention to Harry's words. He was looking at a notice someone had pasted up on the post next to the bars. It read: HEALTHY HEART RUNATHON TEAMS, ATTENTION. PRIZE DAY. SCHOOL GYMNASIUM. The date given was the first day of school after spring vacation.

Pete read it all aloud: "The team whose five members total the greatest number of laps will win a plaque for its classroom."

Harry grinned and said, "I bet we win."

"Wait a minute," Sara said. She was still looking at the notice. "There's more."

"Where?" said Pete.

"Here at the bottom."

She read it over his shoulder. "Please note: No team will be eligible for award unless every team member is present."

Everybody looked at Mishmash.

"Oh brother!" said Sara.

"You mean I've been running a whole week for nothing?" said Adele.

Harry sat down heavily on the bench. "Well, that does it. We're finished. Kaput. Done with."

Pete kept staring at the notice. "We'll just have to take Mishmash to school with us that morning."

Harry stood up again. "We'll what?"

"We can't take a dog to school!" said Adele.

Pete turned around and regarded his teammates. "All it says," he said slowly and clearly, "is that all five members must be present. That's all it says."

10

On the last day of the runathon, runners crowded the schoolground. All the dogs in the neighborhood came to run back and forth across the field and bark at the runners. Nobody paid any attention. Hardly anybody noticed the big black dog who answered to the name of Mishmash.

Mishmash tagged after the heels of the runners who had brought cookies to munch and candy bars to nibble. He ran with his nose to the ground, picking up the crumbs. Every time he made a complete circle, Pete filled in one half-mile square next to the dog's name on the team's scorecard. He filled in so many squares that he reached the end of the row and had to start on another.

———

No one saw Mishmash walking through the back door of the gym on Prize Day. No one turned around to see Pete's team enter. With all the stirring and shuffling, no one noticed the dog sitting on the last chair in the last row. Everyone was too busy whispering and pointing to the prizes displayed on the table in front of the platform.

Feet stamped and hands clapped when the principal entered the gym. He came to the front of the room and smiled and bowed, then raised his hands to stop the noise. The teachers began to shush everyone. Pretty soon there was more shushing than there was clapping.

Principal Wright cleared his throat, coughed behind his hand, and stepped up on a box so everyone could see him. "I know you're all anxious to get back to your classrooms," he began.

"Oh brother," breathed Sara. Mishmash yawned.

"So I'll get right to our purpose for being here today — the award giving."

Everybody clapped.

Mr. Wright held up his hand for silence. "First I want to tell you," he said, "how proud I am of the single and combined efforts of everyone in this school, including the teachers, who have made our Healthy Heart program such a success. And I want to say congratulations to every one of you! For starting something very good for yourselves. Every participant, whether an award winner or not, has proved that he or she is on the way to becoming physically fit."

Pete saw Wanda sitting in one of the front rows. He'd know the back of her head anywhere — the way her hair stuck up on top, and the way her ears stuck out. He was a little surprised when the head turned and he saw that it wasn't Wanda after all.

Mr. Wright began to announce the winners. There seemed to be a great many awards: one for the first grade, and one for the second grade, and one for the third grade. Then the proceedings stopped while the third-grade teacher stood up and called her teams to the front to sing a song she had written. It had a lot of "hail, hails" and heavy panting. All the teachers clapped. Then came the fourth-grade prize, and more speeches.

Sara poked at Pete. Mishmash had slid down to the floor and was snoozing under the seat. Pete was frowning at Mishmash when the next prize was announced. He didn't even hear it the first time. He didn't have to hear it, because there was Wanda walking up to the principal to receive the fifth-grade award.

Wanda!

Pete heard Harry say "Oooof."

Wanda's team was the winner. Wanda's name would be on the plaque. Her team was screeching and yelling. Mr. Wright was shaking her hand. Miss Patch was smiling at Wanda, her teeth sticking out so far that there were two dents in her cheeks. Glumly Pete stared down at his shoes.

The principal was yelling for attention. "We have one more prize!" he shouted over the noise. Everyone quieted down. He was holding something up. It was a leather string, and at the end of it dangled a gold medal, or something that looked like gold. It caught the light coming through the screened windows high up on the wall of the gym. It glinted.

"Ahhhhhhh," everyone murmured in surprise.

"This," said the principal, "is for the single team member who has individually logged more laps than anyone on any team in the whole school."

Pete sat forward, holding his breath. He had run more miles than Wanda. He knew he had.

Mr. Wright picked up his paper, set his glasses on his nose, and waited until all the shuffling stopped. Every eye turned to the front of the room, and every breath seemed to stop.

"I am pleased to announce that this gold medal goes to the team member whose name is —" Principal Wright looked down at his paper. He lifted the paper up closer to his eyes — "*Mishmash?!*"

The name rang out over the gymnasium. Pete gasped. A flash of black passed under his feet and out into the aisle. It streaked up between the rows of seats, leaped toward the principal, and stood there panting. A big black dog with his tail wagging through the air and his mouth stretched into a very wide grin stood before the principal.

"*Mishmash!*" shrieked Miss Patch.

Mishmash turned to face the audience. He gave one loud bark, turned again, thrust his head through the circle of ribbon dangling from Mr. Wright's frozen hands, and, with the medal flashing on his black chest, galloped back down the aisle.

11

———

"Mishmash is out playing," Miss Patch said when Pete came to her door. On her face was a pleased smile, and on her feet a pair of new jogging shoes. The shoestrings were tied in big floppy bows.

"Ever since Mishmash won that gold medal, he's been the most popular dog on the block," she told Pete. "He's so popular he's hardly taken time to eat."

"Popular?"

"The first-grade class came to have their pictures taken with him this morning. Yesterday it was the third graders. And now he's off with Wanda.

"*Wanda!*"

"They've become quite good friends," said Miss Patch.

Pete stumbled a little as he went down the walk and out the gate.

"Come back tomorrow," the teacher called after him. "I'm sure he'll be home for a little while tomorrow."

———

"There's milk for you on the kitchen table," Mrs. Peters said as Pete came through the back door. "And you can help yourself to some of those cookies." She went upstairs.

Pete sat down at the table, nibbled a cookie, and drank some of the milk. There was a hollow feeling inside him. He tried to fill it with cookies.

Pete remembered how Mishmash used to come running around from the back of the teacher's house whenever he came to see him. How he used to come to a skidding stop in front of Pete, and yip and yap and stand up on his hind legs and flap his long red tongue across Pete's face. How he used to act as if Wanda weren't even there. Wanda.

Wanda and Mishmash.

Pete remembered Mishmash inviting his dog friends to a party when Miss Patch was in Europe. He remembered that Mishmash never liked to play alone. The hollow place inside him felt bigger than ever. Pete stuffed another cookie into his mouth.

He remembered all of a sudden that he had left Mishmash to play alone a lot when he became captain of his running team.

Pete swallowed and reached for another. The plate was almost empty. Pete thought of Mishmash stuffing himself with food. He stared at the cookie in his hand for a long time before he put it back on the plate.

12

"I'm not giving any autographs today," Wanda shouted at Pete as she came out of her house the next day. She had a camera slung around her neck, and was carrying a plate covered with old Christmas wrapping paper. "I've already given so many autographs that I've got writer's cramp."

"I don't want your autograph," Pete shouted back. "What would I do with your autograph?"

She smiled. "Yes, I can see why you can't understand why everyone wants my autograph. It's not easy to accept defeat," she said wisely.

"You only got a plaque," he reminded her. "Mishmash got the gold medal."

She sniffed. "Mishmash is persona non grata around here, if you know what I mean."

Pete didn't have to know what she meant. Even winning a gold medal hadn't made Mishmash any more welcome in the neighborhood. Nobody understood Mishmash the way he did. Pete grimaced, feeling an odd pain.

"My mother says if she sees him hanging around here again, medal or no medal, she's going to call the dog catcher."

"That's only because she still thinks he snatched her Weight Watchers dinners."

"And it's also because our burglar alarm keeps ringing half a dozen times a night," said Wanda.

"What has that got to do with Mishmash?"

Wanda gave him a pitying glance. "It's safe to assume that any unusual circumstance has something to do with Mishmash."

Pete didn't bother to disagree.

"Anyway, you can come with me if you want to," said Wanda.

Pete snorted. "I'm not going anywhere with you. I'm going to see Mishmash."

"That's where I'm going myself. I'm taking him a present." She raised the package she was carrying. "Dog brownies."

Pete laughed. "Whoever heard of dog brownies?"

"It's an original recipe," she said with pride. "It's got peanuts and molasses and pickle juice."

Pete clutched his stomach. "Wagggghhhhhhh!"

"Mrs. Barnes said it's the most interesting brownie recipe she's ever heard of."

"Claggggggghhhhhhhhhh!" Pete clutched both hands to his throat.

"Mrs. Anderson said it's almost as unusual as her zucchini cookies."

Making strangling sounds, Pete staggered along for a step or two.

"You don't have to like them," she said with a sniff. "They're for Mishmash. He's going to be delighted. It's probably the best present anybody ever gave him." She began to hurry along.

Pete walked a little faster.

"I'm planning to submit my original recipe to

the Flour Mills Bake-Off contest. I bet they've never had a recipe for dog brownies before."

"That's certainly a fact," said Pete.

"I'm going to take a picture of Mishmash smacking his lips. I'll probably win first prize," she said modestly.

Pete didn't even bother to respond to that.

"I tried it on all the kids in the neighborhood. They simply loved it."

"Kids aren't dogs," Pete heard himself say.

"Don't tell that to Mishmash," said Wanda. "He doesn't know that kids and dogs belong to different categories. He thinks kids and dogs are one and the same. The only difference he sees between kids and dogs is that some of them wear socks."

Pete thought of Mishmash sitting on a chair and sleeping on a bed and taking a bubble bath. For some reason a lump was rising in his throat.

"When I win my prize in the bake-off contest, I'm going to put it in my trophy room."

"What trophy room?"

"I'll probably open it to visitors on Mondays and Wednesdays," said Wanda thoughtfully. "For a fee, that is — unless you're accompanied by a VIP. If you're accompanied by a Very Important Person, you get in free."

Pete stopped listening.

"But you can't count Mishmash. He's one VIP who won't get past our front door."

Pete tried to laugh. But somehow the laugh came out strangled.

Wanda gave him a quick glance. "You mustn't feel bad just because you didn't win anything. We can't all be winners."

Pete moved ahead a little faster. He wished he had thought of bringing Mishmash a present too.

Pete opened Miss Patch's gate and walked up to her front door. Mishmash's gold medal was lying on the porch. Pete picked it up.

"Come in," said Miss Patch, smiling.

"Hi, Mishmash," Wanda said, holding up her gift. "I brought you something."

The dog stood up on his hind legs and flapped

his tongue over Wanda's face.

"Yacccccch!" Wanda stuck out her elbows and pushed him away.

Pete put the gold medal down on the table. "Hi, Mishmash," he said, but part of the name got caught in his throat.

Mishmash grabbed the medal and went out the door and down the steps. He crossed the lawn to a spot near the fence, dropped the medal onto the soft earth, and quickly covered it up.

"You'd better come right back in here," Miss Patch shouted. "You've got company."

Mishmash came scrambling back.

"Wipe your feet," Miss Patch reminded.

Mishmash stopped at the doorway, shuffled his feet over the old mat, and trotted in. Then he picked up his hind leg, kicked the door closed, and came to the middle of the room.

Pete hadn't known Mishmash could do that. "Good dog," Pete said, patting him on the head.

Mishmash looked surprised. Pete dropped down to his knees and locked his arms around the dog's body. "I really love you, Mishmash," he whispered against one of the long black ears.

Mishmash blinked.

"He doesn't stuff himself anymore," Miss Patch said proudly. "He's not gaining any more weight, and he's stopped watching television all the time."

"It's probably all those Weight Watchers dinners," said Wanda, taking the credit for herself. "Once you learn to eat right, you don't overeat all the time."

A "whiffffffffff" came out of the dog's mouth.

Pete felt like laughing. He knew why Mishmash was his old happy self again. And it had nothing to do with diet food, or hypnosis, or even with running around the track.

Wanda put the plate of dog brownies down in front of Mishmash. Mishmash stuck his nose into the plate and sniffed.

"This is going to be a prize winner," Wanda said importantly as she held the camera up to her eyes. "Okay, Mishmash. *Smile.*"

Mishmash stepped forward. He stepped right

on top of the brownies. Obligingly he grinned. At Pete.

"Mishmash!" shouted Wanda.

Suddenly Pete felt a little sorry for Wanda. One thing he knew for sure. No matter how many prizes she won, she'd never be first with Mishmash.